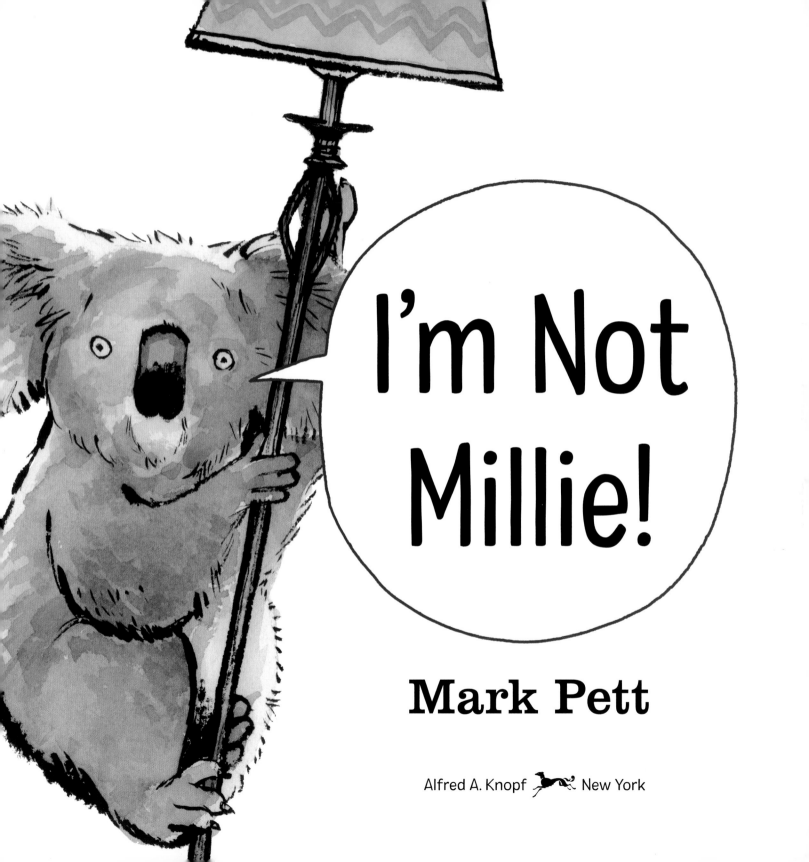

I'm Not Millie!

Mark Pett

Alfred A. Knopf · New York

THIS IS A BORZOI BOOK PUBLISHED BY ALFRED A. KNOPF

Visit us on the Web! rhcbooks.com

Educators and librarians, for a variety of teaching tools, visit us at RHTeachersLibrarians.com

*Library of Congress Cataloging-in-Publication Data*
Names: Pett, Mark, author.
Title: I'm not Millie / Mark Pett.
Other titles: I am not Millie
Description: First edition. | New York : Alfred A. Knopf, [2019] | Summary: Someone is causing
a lot of trouble during and after supper, but Millie is certainly not the guilty one.
Identifiers: LCCN 2018008092 (print) | LCCN 2018015702 (ebook) | ISBN 978-1-101-93793-8 (trade) |
ISBN 978-1-101-93794-5 (lib. bdg.) | ISBN 978-1-101-93795-2 (ebook)
Subjects: | CYAC: Behavior—Fiction. | Identity—Fiction. | Humorous stories.
Classification: LCC PZ7.P4478 (ebook) | LCC PZ7.P4478 Iam 2019 (print) |
DDC [E]—dc23
The text of this book is set in 44-point Clarendon and 36-point Colby Narrow.
The illustrations were created using India ink and watercolor.

MANUFACTURED IN CHINA

November 2019
10 9 8 7 6 5 4 3 2 1
First Edition

For Millie